Mister Tinker
in Oz

Mister Tinker
in Oz

By James Howe
Illustrated by David Rose

Random House New York

This one's just for Joanna Lynn Carver.
—J.H.

Text copyright © 1985 by Random House, Inc. Illustrations copyright © 1985 by David S. Rose. All rights reserved under International and Pan-American Copyright Conventions. Published in the United States by Random House, Inc., New York, and simultaneously in Canada by Random House of Canada Limited, Toronto.

Library of Congress Cataloging in Publication Data: Howe, James. Mister Tinker in Oz. SUMMARY: Dorothy leads Ezra Tinker, an inventor from the moon, to the Land of Oz to save the life of Tik-Tok, the mechanical man. 1. Children's stories, American. [1. Fantasy]   I. Rose, David S., 1947–   ill.   II. Title. III. Title: Mister Tinker in Oz.   PZ7.H83727Mi   1985   [Fic]   84-16105   ISBN: 0-394-87038-7 (trade); 0-394-97038-1 (lib. bdg.)

Manufactured in the United States of America 1 2 3 4 5 6 7 8 9 0

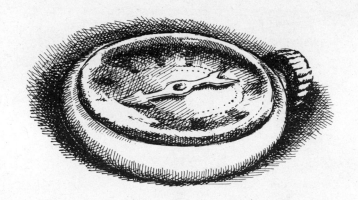

Contents

Mister Tinker
Drops In

"Dear oh dear oh dear." Aunt Em put down her knitting and shook her head. "I can't remember when I've heard such a terrible wind," she said. "Just listen to it howl."

"It's not the wind that bothers me," Uncle Henry remarked, knocking the ashes from his pipe. "It's the creaking of that gate."

Aunt Em nodded. "Dorothy," she said. "Oh, Dorothy, dear."

The young girl did not hear her aunt speak at

first. Curled up in a worn friendly chair before the fire, she was lost in her dreams.

"Dorothy, run outside and fasten the gate. That's a good girl."

"The gate?" Dorothy said, rubbing the dreams from her eyes. "Oh, yes, of course, Aunt Em."

"But do hurry back in," cautioned Aunt Em, returning to her knitting. "It's a cruel wind that would as soon blow you down as keep you standing."

But to Dorothy, who had once been carried off by a cyclone, the wind meant adventure more than cruelty. As she struggled to close the willful gate, she thought about the wonderful adventures she had had far from her home in Kansas.

"I do wish I could go back to Oz," she said aloud. "I wish I could see my friends in the Emerald City."

She was startled from her thoughts when she beheld in the field across the road a long ladder descending from the sky. She could not tell where it came from nor what it was leaning against, but it was certainly the longest ladder she had ever seen. And then, by the light of the moon, she beheld an even queerer sight. There, coming down the ladder, was the figure of a man, clothed in a billowing robe and a tall, peaked hat.

What a peculiar thing, Dorothy thought as the odd-looking man stumbled across the field and approached her. He was terribly tall and his quick, jerky movements made it seem that he was held together more by wire and wishes than skin and bones. He came to a sudden halt in the middle of the road before her.

"Is this the Land of Ev?" he asked.

"No," Dorothy replied. "This is Kansas. But I have been to Ev. Why do you want to go there? Who are you? Are you a wizard?"

"I'm not a wizard," said the man. "I am something much more down to moon . . . excuse me, I mean 'down to earth.' I am an inventor. Tinker is the name."

From one sleeve of his robe he produced a card and handed it to Dorothy. Upon it were these words:

EZRA P. TINKER

If you need it in a hurry,
But you don't know what it is,
There's no need for further worry:
I'll invent it . . . that's my biz!

Third house past the fourth crater. Moon.
Knock before entering.

"Do you live on the moon?" Dorothy asked.

"Yes," replied Mister Tinker. "That is whence I've come. But the question is not one of *whence* but *whither*. The Land of Ev is whither I go. Or whither I *wish* to go in any event. This is *not* Ev, then?"

Dorothy shook her head. The lanky man in the peaked hat put his hand up his other sleeve and pulled out what appeared to be a pocket watch.

"I don't understand," he muttered. Seeing Dorothy's puzzled expression, he explained. "This watch is also a compass with the unusual ability to direct one to moons, stars, planets, and lands, both real and imagined. I say 'unusual ability' because it is the only one of its kind. I invented it. Now, it is my understanding from this watch that the one-thousand-year guarantee on one of my other inventions is just about up, and if that is so, I must locate it at once and perform whatever is necessary to keep it in operation. Otherwise, I am afraid its life, such as it is, will be over. Kaput! Finito!" Mister Tinker took a breath, then added, "The invention of which I speak is a certain mechanical man named Tik-Tok—"

"Tik-Tok!" cried Dorothy. "Why, he's a friend of mine!"

"Is he? Well, then, perhaps you can help me find him. You see, I invented Tik-Tok when I lived in the Land of Ev, and that is where I believe he is still."

"Oh, Mister Tinker," Dorothy said. "Tik-Tok is no longer in the Land of Ev. He is in the Land of Oz."

"In Oz?" said Mister Tinker, much surprised.

"Yes," replied Dorothy. "In the Emerald City."

"Well, I'll be. Then I must go to the Emerald City at once! But how shall I get there? I could set my compass-watch, but if it brought me to Kansas when I meant to go to Ev, it must not be working properly."

"I know the way," said Dorothy. "And I was just this minute wishing I could return to Oz and see my friends once again. I'll go with you if you'd like."

Mister Tinker said, "Your idea's not a bad one. But I must hurry, for the sands of Tik-Tok's life, if you will allow me to turn a phrase poetical, are in great danger of running out. Can you leave at once, my dear?"

Dorothy glanced behind her at Toto's face in the parlor window. She could see the smoke rising from Uncle Henry's pipe and the glint of Aunt

Ein's knitting needles in the lamplight. She knew they would worry when she didn't return, but, oh, how she wanted to go to Oz. And when she thought of her poor friend, Tik-Tok . . .

"Yes," she said, making up her mind in that instant. "I'll go with you. But I mustn't stay away too long."

"Whatever you wish," replied Mister Tinker. "Now, let us be on our way." And the inventor in the tall, peaked hat and the billowy robe reached up his sleeve once more as if to pull from it the means of transporting them to the Land of Oz.

Which is exactly what he did.

Small As a Speck

"What's in the envelope?" asked Dorothy, when she saw what Mister Tinker had drawn from his sleeve.

"Nothing, my dear," replied the inventor. Then he added, with a wink, "Nothing *yet,* that is. By the bye, as long as we are to be traveling companions, might I call you by a name other than 'my dear'?"

"You may call me Dorothy."

"Then, Dorothy it shall be," said Mister Tinker.

He then reached up under his hat and pulled out a sort of telescope. "Now, before we use this," he said, "we must address the envelope." And with a pencil he wrote "To Oz."

"Don't you need a stamp?" Dorothy asked.

Mister Tinker regarded the girl solemnly, placed the envelope on the ground, and gave it a stamp with his foot.

"That should do it," he declared.

"Now you must lick the flap," Dorothy suggested.

"Heavens, no," replied Mister Tinker, strangely alarmed, "we mustn't do that. Else, how would we get inside? Now, let me see, it's been some time since I've used my Speckoscope. Hmm, I believe . . . ah, yes, I have it."

Ezra P. Tinker stuck the curiously named telescope in a knothole in the gate and instructed Dorothy to stand back. He then tucked the envelope under the heel of her shoe and told her that at the count of three, she should gaze through the Speckoscope and that he would do the same from where he stood.

"One . . . two . . . three!" he called out.

Dorothy bent over, looked through the telescope, and saw a teeny, tiny Mister Tinker looking back at her.

"How do I appear?" Mister Tinker cried.

"Small," replied Dorothy.

"So do you, my dear," Mister Tinker called back. Dorothy felt herself grow smaller and smaller until she was no bigger than a speck. *So that's why it's called a Speckoscope,* she thought.

She heard Mister Tinker shout, "Hurry inside the envelope, Dorothy. I'll be right there to join you."

Dorothy did as she was told, but no sooner was she inside than the envelope lifted off the ground. She threw herself down, hoping to hold it in place. But Dorothy now weighed no more than a good-night kiss and so her efforts were quite in vain.

"Mister Tinker!" she cried in alarm.

"I'm coming!" called out Mister Tinker.

But his voice grew fainter and fainter, and Dorothy could no longer see him as the wind lifted the envelope higher than the treetops. She shuddered to think that she was quite alone; that,

indeed, there was little hope of seeing Mister Tinker again.

"Oh, my," she said. "What's to become of me?"

The combined weight of Dorothy and the envelope was so slight that she felt not a jolt, not a bump, not so much as a hiccup when she landed some hours later. She crawled to the open flap of the envelope and peered out. Tall green towers surrounded her, some flat and sharp-edged, some round and smooth.

What strange buildings, Dorothy thought, noticing that they had no windows.

Just then, she heard the sound of babies crying. At least, that's what she *thought* she heard. She jumped down from the edge of the envelope flap and looked about. A tiny head bearing a mop of yellow hair poked itself out from behind one of the towers. Wiping the tears from its eyes, the creature, who looked very much like a human baby, asked, "Who are *you?*"

"I'm Dorothy," replied the girl in a soft voice. "And who are you?"

"I'm lost!" the baby said, and began to sob fiercely once again.

Suddenly many other heads, much like the first, popped out from behind green towers. They, too, were crying.

"Are you crying just because you're lost?" asked Dorothy. "I'm lost too, but you don't see me crying, do you?"

"You're a big girl," said one, between sniffles. "We're just Widdlebits."

"We crawled away from the Widdlebit picnic and don't know how to get back," said another. "And now we're in the land of the Shiny Bellies, who will eat us all up as soon as they know we're here."

"Will you take care of us?" asked a third. And creeping and crawling as fast as they could, the Widdlebits made their way to Dorothy and huddled around her.

"Oh, dear," said Dorothy, "I wish I could help you. But I don't even know what a Shiny Belly is. And I'm sure I wouldn't know what to do if one came along to eat you. Besides, I must try and get to Oz."

Suddenly all of the Widdlebits stopped crying. "You're *in* Oz," one said after a moment.

19

"I am?" said Dorothy, surprised.

"Yes, you're in Winkie Country."

"Then, to get to the Emerald City," said Dorothy, overjoyed at this bit of news, "all I need to do is walk east. For Winkie Country is in the western part of Oz, is it not?"

The Widdlebits nodded and looked up at her sadly. "You're not going to leave us, are you?" asked one, tears glistening in his long yellow lashes.

Just as Dorothy was trying to decide what to do, a terrifying screech announced the arrival of the Shiny Bellies. The Widdlebits hid their faces, and Dorothy looked about her. From every direction came huge, shiny black monsters. Their eyes lit up as they spied this group of juicy Widdlebits

and the particularly tasty-looking young girl in its midst. They made Dorothy think of ants at a picnic. And it was then that she realized that that was exactly what they were.

Dorothy had forgotten how tiny she was. Now she understood that the tall green towers around her were blades of grass and stalks of dandelions. And the Shiny Bellies were nothing more than common ants. She had never been frightened of ants before. But, of course, she had never been smaller than an ant before, either.

The Shiny Bellies, who had formed a circle around them, suddenly reared up on their back legs. Their heads were almost as high as the towers of grass. They trumpeted triumphantly.

Dorothy closed her eyes.

3

Julius QuickScissors
to the Rescue

"Zzzzzip! Zzzzzip! Zipzipzipzipzipzzzzip!"
The sound of something whizzing through the air seemed to come from right above Dorothy's head. She opened her eyes and watched in amazement as hundreds of grass towers fell and the grinning heads of the Shiny Bellies flew off their bodies and tumbled to the ground. The whimpering Widdlebits held tightly to Dorothy and to each other, not daring to look up and see what all the commotion was about.

The earth shook as something crashed against a rock nearby.

The Widdlebits peeked out from behind their trembling hands.

"Why," said Dorothy, staring at the object which had just landed, "it's a giant pair of scissors. That is, it is a *normal* pair of scissors that *appears* giant because I am so small."

The Widdlebits stopped their whimpering as Dorothy led them to investigate.

It was indeed a pair of scissors, and on its side were engraved these words:

> The Fastest-Acting Scissors in the
> Whole, Wide Universe
> Will *Cut* Your Work in Half
> and Then Some . . .
> Julius QuickScissors, by Name
> Shear Perfection Guaranteed
> **Ezra P. Tinker, Inventor**
> **Moon**

"Mister Tinker!" cried Dorothy. "I'll bet he sent these scissors to bring me to him. Why, perhaps he's in the Emerald City already."

"Are you leaving us?" one of the Widdlebits asked, starting once again to cry.

"I can't leave you here," Dorothy said, thinking aloud. "There may be more Shiny Bellies around."

"Shiny Bellies, Shiny Bellies," echoed the Widdlebits, shaking as they uttered the dreaded name.

"Take us with you," said one. "We've never been anywhere but Widdlebit Forest. We want to go to Em'rald City!"

"Em'rald City . . . Em'rald City," the Widdlebits chanted.

"I don't know what else I *can* do," Dorothy said. She spied Shiny Bellies lurking among the grass and dandelion towers. "You may come with me. But hurry, hurry."

Dorothy and the Widdlebits crawled up a bent piece of grass onto the scissors handle. They were all so tiny that they were able to slip into a scratch in Julius QuickScissors's side made by his encounter with the rock.

"Zzzz . . . zzzz . . . zzzippp . . . zipzipzipzip-zzZZZZZZZZIIPPPP!"

They were off! They whizzed across the land

so fast that the flowers and grass around them became nothing but a blur of yellow and green.

"Ah, Julius!" Mister Tinker cried some time later when he spotted the scissors flying toward him. "I've been wondering where you've been off to. You really are the most mischievous of all my inventions. Come here at once!"

Julius QuickScissors came to rest in Mister Tinker's palm.

"Mister Tinker!" Dorothy shouted.

"Mister Tinker! Mister Tinker!" echoed the Widdlebits.

But since Mister Tinker had returned to his former size, he could not hear their tiny voices at all.

"Oh, dear," he said, looking carefully at the errant pair of scissors. "It seems you've suffered a nasty scratch, Julius. Well, I'll have that fixed up in a hurry." And he reached up one of his sleeves and brought forth a bottle. As if she were reading a huge billboard, Dorothy made out the words *Wishful Fixing* on the label.

"Now," Mister Tinker said as he held a dropper over the scratch in Julius QuickScissors's side, "you must *wish* that scratch to disappear, Julius. Otherwise, this lotion of mine will do no good." He read aloud the instructions on the side of the bottle. " 'Mix one drop with one wish.' And please, dear friend, wish *hard* because there is only one drop left. Quite thoughtless of me to have left home with such a small supply, but one doesn't always think clearly when one is in a rush."

"We're going to drown!" cried one of the Widdlebits. But Dorothy realized that they would drown only if they *wished* to. For she sensed that this lotion of Mister Tinker's had the power to make their wishes, whatever they might be, come true.

"Widdlebits!" Dorothy shouted. "We must all wish to be *big*. It is the only way we will be saved. Now, all of you, think as hard as you can and as big as you can!"

The drop of Wishful Fixing Lotion fell with a great *ker-plop*. When Dorothy shook the wetness from her, she found herself standing next to Mister Tinker. And all about them were creeping, crawling, *normal-sized* babies in yellow diapers. Dorothy could not help noticing that among the

babies there was also a large sheepdog.

"It's Dorothy!" exclaimed Mister Tinker. "Wherever did you come from, my dear? And who are these . . . er . . . young people with you?"

"They're Widdlebits," replied Dorothy. "At least, most of them are. I'm not sure about the dog."

"That must be Homer," one of the Widdlebits said. "He always wanted to be a dog."

Mister Tinker shook his head. "I am stunned to find you standing before me, my dear."

"Didn't you send the scissors to find me?" asked Dorothy.

"I wish I could say I did," replied Mister Tinker. "I'm afraid the truth is that I had taken him out of my pocket to clip my toenails. A most odious task. It was my aversion to clipping toenails that caused me to invent Julius QuickScissors in the first place. To get the loathsome job over with quickly, don't you see? I had just removed my shoes when Julius took off for the hills. I don't understand it," he said. "My inventions just don't seem to be working properly at all."

Dorothy was about to ask Mister Tinker how

he had managed to come to Oz when she heard a loud ringing noise.

"Oh, dear!" cried Mister Tinker, reaching into a sleeve and pulling out his compass-watch. "The one-thousand-year guarantee on Tik-Tok has just run out! This is dreadful, this is more than dreadful, this is more than more than dreadful! I must get to Tik-Tok at once. But how can I when I still don't know how to reach the Emerald City?"

"Look!" Dorothy cried, pointing to a sign. It read:

To the Emerald City—
Just the other side of the Bottomless Swamp.
Not far . . . if you make it.

"The Bottomless Swamp," Mister Tinker said. "How on moon . . . I mean, how on earth . . . shall we get across?"

Dorothy looked at Mister Tinker sternly. "Now, Mister Tinker," she said, "we are very near the Emerald City and we *must* get there to save Tik-Tok. Be *positive*! When we reach the Bottomless Swamp, you will think of a way to get across. You *are* an inventor, after all."

"I don't feel much like an inventor *these* days," Mister Tinker said sadly. "But I suppose you are right. We must be positive."

And so Dorothy, Mister Tinker, Julius QuickScissors, the Widdlebits, and a sheepdog named Homer started down the road toward the Emerald City.

The Bottomless Swamp

Soon they reached the Bottomless Swamp. A sign greeted them.

The Bottomless Swamp
No Swimming, Picnicking, or Littering Allowed
Watch Out for Wumpguppies

"Wumpguppies?" said Dorothy. "What do you suppose they are?"

"It is said," came an unseen voice as full of

31

creaks as attic stairs, "that the Wumpguppies possess the bodies of fish and the heads of creatures so ugly that any person unfortunate enough to look at one is guaranteed to faint on the spot. They live in the Bottomless Swamp but are capable of leaping from its waters and scaring the daylights out of anyone passing by."

"Who is speaking?" Dorothy asked.

"Just a foolish old woman," replied the voice. And then through an opening in a large tree trunk, there appeared someone who looked very much like a gypsy. To the great delight of the Widdlebits, the bells and beads and baubles she wore created quite a delicious racket as she walked toward the group.

"Is there a way across the Bottomless Swamp?" inquired Mister Tinker.

"Just take the Rickety-Rackety Bridge," replied the old woman, pointing a spindly hand. "As you can see, it's not far from there to the other side."

Dorothy and the others looked in the direction the old woman pointed. There they saw a narrow wooden bridge spanning the Bottomless Swamp.

And in the distance they could make out green towers gleaming in the sun.

"It's the Emerald City!" cried Dorothy. "We're not far at all. Thank you, Miss . . . er . . . Missus . . . um . . . "

"Princess Astoria," replied the old woman, lifting her chin. "I am one of seven sisters. *They* are all queens. But because I was the last born, they would not allow me to be a queen as well. At a tender age I set off for the Emerald City to petition the Wizard to grant me my right to queenhood. When I reached the Bottomless Swamp, I stopped to rest. An old man told me about the Wumpguppies, much as I have told you, and I was too frightened to continue on my journey. For several days we watched for the Wumpguppies, but none flew out of the water. Finally the old man said, 'This is nonsense! I am going to the Emerald City.' He started across the bridge. Suddenly a swarm of Wumpguppies leaped from beneath the swamp's surface and so startled the old man that he could not help but look right at them. He fainted dead away, falling off the bridge and into the Bottomless

Swamp. For all I know he is falling through its murky waters still." She stopped and sighed. "I put up the sign then to warn others, and have lived here at the water's edge ever since."

Dorothy regarded Princess Astoria with sympathy. But she noticed that Mister Tinker was tapping his foot, and Julius QuickScissors, hanging at Mister Tinker's side, was snapping open and shut, indicating, she thought, his desire for the old woman to cut her story short.

"I am sorry for your trouble," said Dorothy then, "but we must hurry on to the Emerald City. Our friend Tik-Tok's very life may be in danger, you see, so we haven't a moment to lose."

"But what about the Wumpguppies?" cried one of the Widdlebits.

"Wumpguppies. . .Wumpguppies," the others chanted.

"They're right," said Dorothy to Mister Tinker. "We must do something about the Wumpguppies. Otherwise, we will fall into the Bottomless Swamp."

Mister Tinker sat down on a rock and thought and thought.

All at once he cried, "I have it!" He reached up
one of his sleeves and brought out two small cubes.
"What luck that I thought to bring with me my
patented full-length folding mirrors."

"What good will mirrors do us?" Dorothy
asked, puzzled.

"Just hear me out, my dear," said Mister Tinker
patiently. "Princess Astoria has said that the
Wumpguppies are so ugly that anyone who looks
at them will faint dead away. Is that not so?"

Princess Astoria nodded.

"Therefore, if we hold the mirrors on either side of us as we pass over the Rickety-Rackety Bridge," Mister Tinker continued, unfolding the two mirrors, "the Wumpguppies will see themselves when they jump out of the water, and will be so frightened by their own reflections, *they* will be the ones to faint! And we will be quite safe."

Dorothy and the Widdlebits marveled at this bit of cunning and concluded from it that Mister Tinker was indeed an outstanding inventor. But Princess Astoria had her doubts.

"One or two of you may be able to hide behind those mirrors, but how will the rest of you avoid looking at the Wumpguppies?" she said.

Mister Tinker puzzled over this for a moment. "Dorothy and I will lead the way," he said, "holding the mirrors. The Widdlebits will form a line behind us, each holding on to the one before. They will keep their eyes closed, and we shall lead them safely to the other side."

"It just might work," Princess Astoria said. "And if that is so . . . oh, my friends, may I go with you? After all these years, this may be my chance to get to the Emerald City. May I go with you, please?"

"All right," said Mister Tinker, "but we must leave this minute. Are you ready to go?"

"Oh, my," Princess Astoria replied excitedly. "I've been waiting so long, how could I not be ready?" And she clasped her hands together, causing her bracelets to jingle and jangle and the Widdlebits to laugh delightedly.

As the Rickety-Rackety Bridge jerked this way and that beneath their every step, they came to understand how it had gotten its name. The Widdlebits were afraid to close their eyes, but Dorothy convinced them to do so for their own good. Princess Astoria, who was the last in line, sang happy songs as they went along to take their minds off their worries. Her lovely voice, though cracked with age, comforted them all.

But what *other* sounds they heard! As they inched their way across the bridge, the splashing on both sides of them made it seem as if the swamp were exploding.

"Don't look!" Mister Tinker warned Dorothy.

"Just hold tight to the mirrors and keep moving ahead."

The Wumpguppies, intent on terrifying the travelers, leaped up out of the swamp with grimaces on their grotesque faces. But when they saw their reflections in Mister Tinker's folding mirrors, they succeeded only in terrifying themselves. Of course, there were so many of the awful creatures that no sooner had one jumped up, seen its image, and fallen back into the murky waters than another leaped up to replace it.

All at once Homer, who had apparently been left behind, bounded onto the Rickety-Rackety Bridge. The Widdlebits jumped in fear. And Dorothy and Mister Tinker were so startled that they *dropped* the mirrors into the bottomless waters. Fortunately they thought to close their eyes immediately, for the Wumpguppies took advantage of the moment to jump up in great numbers—and all would have been lost if it weren't for the fact that everyone (even Homer, who remembered at the last moment) had their eyes shut.

No one said a word to Homer. They knew he

was not used to being a sheepdog. And even if he were, sheepdogs could not be expected to do anything but bound.

The Widdlebits grew more and more frightened, whimpering at first, then sobbing loudly.

"Perhaps we could just crawl the rest of the way with our eyes closed," Dorothy suggested to Mister Tinker.

"I'm afraid the Widdlebits aren't going to go anywhere, carrying on the way they are," Mister Tinker replied.

"Could you sing to them?" Dorothy called out to Princess Astoria. "Your singing seemed to calm them before. Do you know a lullaby?"

"Well, I . . . I do recall one, yes. Though it's been many years since I've heard it sung. I'll try to remember it."

Now, when Princess Astoria began to sing this particular lullaby, the oddest thing happened. Dorothy found herself smiling. So did Mister Tinker. And as for the Widdlebits, they stopped crying almost at once. Soon they were cooing and sighing, and before they knew what had happened, they had fallen into a deep sleep.

"That was quite a tune," Mister Tinker commented when Princess Astoria stopped singing.

"It's a lullaby my mother used to sing to me when I was a child," said Princess Astoria. "She told me that it was a lullaby for princesses. For princesses, she said, *not* for queens."

It was then that Dorothy became aware of the great silence around them. "There's no more splashing," she whispered. "The Wumpguppies . . ."

"They must have stopped jumping," said Mister Tinker. "Now, Dorothy, be absolutely still and say not a word. I am going to open my eyes."

"Oh! But you shouldn't—"

"Sshhh, my dear."

And when Mister Tinker opened his eyes he was amazed at what he saw. There, just below the swamp's surface, were the smiling, contented faces of the *sleeping* Wumpguppies. And when he saw them he did not faint.

He poked Dorothy gently. "Open your eyes, Dorothy," he said.

She did and was as amazed by what she saw as he had been. She then whispered to the Widdlebit next to her to wake up and open his eyes and he whispered this to the next and he to the next and so on and on down the line of Widdlebits until Princess Astoria was told to open her eyes. And she in turn told Homer, who until then had been hanging his head in shame.

"They're not so ugly," Dorothy said in wonder.

"Of course not," said Princess Astoria. "They're asleep! Nothing is ugly when it is sleeping."

Princess Astoria began to sing the gentle lullaby once again. The Widdlebits tickled each other's feet to keep themselves from falling asleep. And the band of travelers made its way safely to the far shore of the Bottomless Swamp.

From there they could see the gates of the Emerald City.

5

Trouble in the Emerald City

Just as they were about to make the last leg of their journey, they heard the strangest moaning sound coming from within the high walls of the glittering green city.

"What is it, do you suppose?" asked Dorothy.

"I don't know," replied Mister Tinker, "but from the sound of it, something is wrong in the Emerald City."

It was decided then that Dorothy and Mister Tinker would go on ahead while Princess Astoria stayed behind with the Widdlebits. Homer the sheepdog was to stand watch.

It was with some fear and uncertainty that the little girl from Kansas and the lanky inventor from the moon rang the bell at the gate to the city a few moments later.

"What do you want?" the Guardian of the Gates asked. He was a little man with the saddest face Dorothy had ever seen.

"We wish to enter," replied Dorothy.

The little man shrugged. "Why would anyone want to enter the Emerald City?" he said. But he allowed them to pass and, at their request, led them down the sparkling roads of the city to the palace.

Along the way Dorothy and Mister Tinker noticed that the citizens of the Emerald City were shuffling about wordlessly, lifting their shoulders from time to time, then dropping them with great sighs. When they reached the palace, the little man turned and asked, "Is Princess Ozma expecting you?" Princess Ozma was the ruler of Oz.

"No," Dorothy said. "But she will be glad to see me. We are awfully good friends."

"I doubt she will be glad to see you," he muttered. "She is rarely glad to see anyone these days."

Dorothy and Mister Tinker were led into the grand throne room then. Ozma seemed not to notice them at first. She sat upon her throne in the most melancholy manner. When she did see Dorothy, a tiny smile came to her lips. But then it vanished as quickly as it had appeared.

"Hello, little Dorothy," she said in a weary voice. "I'm so glad you've come. I wish I could be gladder, but this is as glad as I can be. Who is this with you?"

Dorothy introduced Mister Tinker, who bowed deeply to her majesty. Then she asked: "What is wrong, Princess Ozma? Everyone is so sad. What has happened?" Then she had a thought. "Is it Tik-Tok?"

Whereupon, as if he had heard his name being uttered, Tik-Tok, the mechanical man, entered the room with his (and Dorothy's) good friend, the Scarecrow.

"Tik-Tok!" shouted Dorothy and Mister Tinker at once. They ran immediately toward their friend and were quite amazed to discover that he seemed to be just fine.

"Good-ness me," Tik-Tok said in his monotonous voice, "what a sur-prise. Dorothy has come to vis-it. And Mis-ter Tink-er, too. I have not seen my in-ven-tor in many, many years."

"Yes," replied Mister Tinker. "One thousand, to be exact." He showed his watch to Tik-Tok and to the Scarecrow, who had no idea what was

going on. "Your guarantee, Tik-Tok, has run out, and I have come to put you into working order again."

"Oh, my," Tik-Tok said with a somewhat squeaky shake of the head, "there is no need to put *me* in-to work-ing order—though my neck could, per-haps, use a lit-tle oil. My guar-an-tee has many more years to run out. Nine hun-dred, twen-ty, and four years, to be exact. In-deed, I have nev-er felt better."

"Oh, I'm so glad," Dorothy said, with great relief. And then she thought to give a hug both to Tik-Tok and to her dear friend, the Scarecrow. "But aren't you sad?"

"Why should we be?" asked the Scarecrow.

"Everyone else in the Emerald City is," Dorothy answered.

The Scarecrow said then, "But we are not hu-man. So we have no reason to feel sad. And if we did, we would not know how."

Mister Tinker had been studying his watch this whole time. "I don't understand what's wrong with it," he muttered. "I was sure that the one-thousand-year guarantee had run out. And now I have come all this way for no reason."

"Per-haps that is not the case," said Tik-Tok. "As it hap-pens, Oz is in great need of an in-ven-tor at this very mo-ment. Your ar-ri-val here is most for-tu-nate."

Suddenly the same moaning sound heard from outside the gates was heard again. "What *is* that noise?" asked Dorothy.

"It is the sound of unhappiness," the Scarecrow told her. "There is great unhappiness in the Emerald City. No one knows the cause of it. No one knows how to make it go away. Not even I with my superior brains."

"Nor I," said Tik-Tok, "with my sharp me-chan-i-cal mind in per-fect working or-der. But you, Mis-ter Tin-ker, are the fi-nest in-ven-tor ever in-ven-ted."

For the first time Princess Ozma perked up. "Perhaps you," she said, addressing Mister Tinker, "could *invent* some way or some thing that would make us happy once again."

Mister Tinker stared at the ground. "I don't know," he mumbled.

"As the ruler of Oz," said Ozma, "I am most

uncomfortable begging. But just this once, I must. I *beg* you to invent a cure for our unhappiness."

Mister Tinker looked into Ozma's troubled eyes. "May I confer with Dorothy?" he asked.

"By all means," she replied, and she signaled Tik-Tok and the Scarecrow to withdraw. Dorothy and Mister Tinker were left by themselves in a corner of the throne room.

"How can I invent a cure for their unhappiness?" he asked. "Of late, none of my inventions has been working properly. I've lost my touch, don't you see? And when I fail, who knows what

they will do to me in their anger and disappointment?"

Dorothy thought for a moment, and then she spoke. "Mister Tinker," she said, "I am certain that you will succeed. I have my reasons for thinking this, but would rather not tell you just now. I promise you, if you just *try*, you will invent a cure."

Mister Tinker looked into Dorothy's big eyes. "All right," he said, "I'll try. But why I'm agreeing to it, I have no idea."

"That's not important. The important thing is that you *try*."

When Mister Tinker told Ozma of his decision, her eyes lit up. She seemed *almost* happy.

"Whenever you are ready," she said to Mister Tinker, "we shall call everyone into the throne room. And here you will show us your happiness invention."

Mister Tinker swallowed hard and nodded. He declined Ozma's invitation to have something to eat. He did not even wish to stay and visit with Dorothy's friends. What he needed was to go off by himself and think.

6

Mister Tinker's
Happiness Invention

It was almost dusk when Dorothy and the Scarecrow found Mister Tinker gazing out of one of the palace's high windows.

"Oh, Dorothy," he said rather forlornly, "I've thought and I've thought. And I've thought of nothing that will solve our problem. What *is* it that brings people happiness? I keep asking myself. And I conclude that happiness comes from within. If that is so, then what good is any invention of mine?"

Dorothy and the Scarecrow saw Mister Tinker's point, though they wished they didn't.

Then Dorothy asked, "What about your Wishful Fixing Lotion, Mister Tinker? If you put a drop of it on everyone's tongue, and they swallowed it while wishing for happiness, *that* would bring them happiness from within, wouldn't it?"

"Alas," replied the inventor. "I have none left. I used the last drop to fix Julius QuickScissors's scratch."

The Scarecrow scowled. Dorothy frowned. And Mister Tinker heaved a great sigh.

And then an idea found its way into the superior brain of the Scarecrow. What if, he suggested, Mister Tinker were to put nothing but *water* in the bottle while telling everyone that it contained Wishful Fixing Lotion? If they *believed* it was the real thing, wouldn't that be almost as good? Ezra Tinker was reluctant to consider this plan at first, for he did not wish to deceive anyone. But the more he thought about it, the more he saw its appeal.

"It is not truly an invention," he said. "But if it brings happiness, well, that's what really counts."

Dorothy and the Scarecrow nodded their heads.

"I will do it! Let us go at once. I am not at all certain it will work, but we will try. And isn't that what you said really matters, young Dorothy, that we *try*?"

A great multitude gathered in the throne room within moments of Princess Ozma's announcement that a cure for unhappiness had been invented.

Mister Tinker stood in the center of the room and said in a great, booming voice: "Ladies and gentlemen, I have just this afternoon concocted my greatest invention to date. It is a cure for every variety of unhappiness known to man, woman, and beast. Yes, Ezra P. Tinker's Wishful Fixing Lotion will put an end, once and for always, to the Down-in-the-Dumps, the Bluer-than-Blues, the Strangely-Sad-Sorries. Now my assistant, that charming young lass from Kansas, Miss Dorothy Gale, will pass among you and place a drop on the tips of your tongues. At that moment, ladies and gentlemen, make a wish for happiness. Then swallow the drop of Wishful Fixing, and happiness will be yours!"

A great excited murmur ran through the room. Mouths fell open eagerly as Dorothy made her way among the crowd, dropping the powerful lotion (which, of course, was only as powerful as the belief to have it so) on each tongue in turn. When she was finished and everyone had closed their eyes and swallowed, a silence fell upon the room.

All at once the door to the throne room flew open and through it came Princess Astoria, the sheepdog Homer, and the cooing, crawling Widdlebits. When the Widdlebits looked up and saw all the gloomy faces staring down at them, they began to whimper with fright. But then they noticed Tik-Tok and the Scarecrow standing among the crowd, and the sight of this odd-looking pair so surprised and delighted them that they quite forgot their fear and began to smile. And their smiles turned to giggles. And their giggles grew into laughter.

And the strangest thing happened. The people of the Emerald City began to smile too. One rushed forward to tickle a Widdlebit under his chin. He was soon joined by others, and all of

them began uttering sounds and making faces that might under other circumstances have been considered idiotic but, under these circumstances, were seen as signs of great joy.

Mister Tinker could not believe his eyes and ears. On every side of him there was happiness. He felt the touch of Princess Ozma's hand on his shoulder and heard her say, "Congratulations, Mister Tinker. Your invention has worked."

"But . . . but . . . but . . ." stuttered Mister Tinker.

Princess Ozma, whose face was radiant, did not let him finish. "What do you *call* it?" she asked.

"What do I call what?" Mister Tinker said.

"Why, your invention, of course. That sound that is filling the room."

He listened carefully, and then he answered. "Why, I call it laughter."

Ozma nodded. "Laughter," she said. "What a wonderful invention. Now that we have laughter in the Emerald City, I am sure we shall never be unhappy again."

Mister Tinker was quite certain that he was not the inventor of laughter. And he couldn't imagine that the people of the Emerald City had never known laughter before. But then the thought occurred to him that they may have *forgotten* how to laugh. Perhaps long ago a day had passed with no laughter in it. And then another had gone by. And another. And before anyone had realized it, the sound of laughter was lost and forgotten. Mister Tinker shook his head to think that such a thing could have happened.

One person after another rushed up to him

and shook him by the hand, thanking him for his happiness invention. He was not sure what to say in response, but decided that "you're welcome" would do.

That evening there was a great celebration in the palace. All of Dorothy's friends were there— the Scarecrow, Tik-Tok, the Tin Woodman, the Cowardly Lion and the Hungry Tiger, Billina the Yellow Hen, Jack Pumpkinhead, Mr. H. M. Woggle-Bug, T. E., and, oh, so many more.

It was decided then that the Widdlebits would stay and live in the Emerald City, since it was not possible for them to return to their former size or their previous homes. They didn't mind because here in Oz they knew they would always be special.

Princess Astoria was happy to remain in the Emerald City too, though she was disappointed at first when Ozma told her it would be impossible to make her a queen.

"You see," said Ozma, "*I* am a princess and I am the ruler of Oz. How could I allow someone else to be in a higher position than mine?" Seeing the look of disappointment in Astoria's eyes, Ozma named her Empress of the Nursery, a title that pleased Astoria no end. She was satisfied now that all her years of waiting by the edge of the Bottomless Swamp had not been in vain.

As for Mister Tinker, he was proclaimed the First and Only Royal and Official Inventor of Oz and invited to stay and live in the palace itself. How could he refuse such an invitation? Well, naturally, he could not. Besides, he said, now when Tik-Tok's one-thousand-year guarantee *did* run out, he would not have to travel all the way from the moon to repair him.

Everyone in the Emerald City slept well that night, especially the Widdlebits, who were lulled to sleep by Empress Astoria's singing.

In the morning Dorothy said good-bye to all her friends. It was time to return home. But before she left, Mister Tinker asked to speak with her alone.

"You told me yesterday," he said, "that you were certain I would succeed when I was certain I would fail. After all, my inventions were no longer working properly. What was it that made you so sure?"

"I did not believe for a minute that your inventions were not working," replied Dorothy. "They were working just fine, though perhaps not in the ways you had expected. Your compass-watch did not take you to Ev because Tik-Tok was in the Emerald City and you didn't know the way there. So it brought you to me, and I was able to guide you. The envelope flew off without you so that I would find the Widdlebits. Julius QuickScissors didn't cut your toenails, but he did rescue me and the Widdlebits and brought us to you. And your full-length folding mirrors worked just fine until Homer made them fall in the water. But then when the Widdlebits started to cry, Princess . . . I mean, Empress . . . Astoria calmed them with a beautiful song and made the Wumpguppies fall asleep too."

"But what about my watch and Tik-Tok's one-thousand-year guarantee?" asked Mister Tinker.

"Don't you see?" said Dorothy. "You weren't needed to fix Tik-Tok, but you *were* needed to bring happiness here. And if everything that had happened along the way hadn't happened, you wouldn't have been able to do just that."

"So my inventions really *did* work," Mister Tinker said in wonder.

Dorothy nodded and said, "Yes, and you really deserve to be the First and Only Royal and Official Inventor of Oz."

"I want you to have this," said Mister Tinker, pressing something into her hands. "A souvenir, you might say."

"Your watch!" Dorothy said, surprised.

"Yes, I worked all last night trying to fix it,"

said Mister Tinker. "I believe if you just set the compass to Kansas, it will take you there."

Dorothy thanked Mister Tinker, kissed him on the cheek, and set the compass-watch to Kansas. Then she closed her eyes.

When she opened them, she was standing at the gate outside her own house. The wind rushed around her. The sky was dark. She looked down at the watch and saw that it had wound itself back to the exact time she had gone out to fasten the gate in the first place. She realized then that, thanks to Mister Tinker's invention, no time had passed in Kansas.

She ran inside the house.

"Is the gate fastened?" asked Aunt Em, barely looking up from her knitting.

"Yes, Aunt Em," said Dorothy.

Uncle Henry puffed on his pipe. "Just listen to that wind howl," he said.

Dorothy sat in her chair by the fire, tucking her legs under her. Toto jumped up into her lap.

"Why don't you read a story?" suggested Aunt Em. "There's nothing like a good story on a night like this."

Dorothy smiled and said not a word. Then she picked up a book from the table next to her and opened it to the first page.